# RACCOONS DON'T USE SPOONS

**SHARON HANZIK**

ILLUSTRATED BY BOBBI SWITZER

Outskirts Press,
Denver, Colorado

ISBN:     978-1-962313-26-1     (Paperback)
ISBN:     978-1-962313-27-8     (Hardback)
ISBN:     978-1-962313-25-4     (eBook)

Book Ordering Information

Writers Book Fair
99 Wall Street Suite 181
New York, NY, 10005, USA

info@writersbookfair.com
www.writersbookfair.com

Printed in the United States of America

**This book belongs to:**

_______________________________

Raccoons don't use spoons or knives or forks.
They have their own tools, they have what works.

Two little hands like yours and mine
hold on to their food whenever they dine.

They'll eat crayfish, minnows, even frogs.
Or worms they find while digging in logs.

No matter the place, no matter the meal
They can hold on, they can even peel!

TRASH

Campers beware! Lock away your food.
These masked bandits will rob you good!

BREAD
Chips

Zippers and snaps won't hold them back.
They are always ready for a sneak attack!

CHIPS
POP

Able, smart, their learning is quick.

They share with each other every new trick.

If you feed them, there will be regret.
No wild animal makes a good pet!

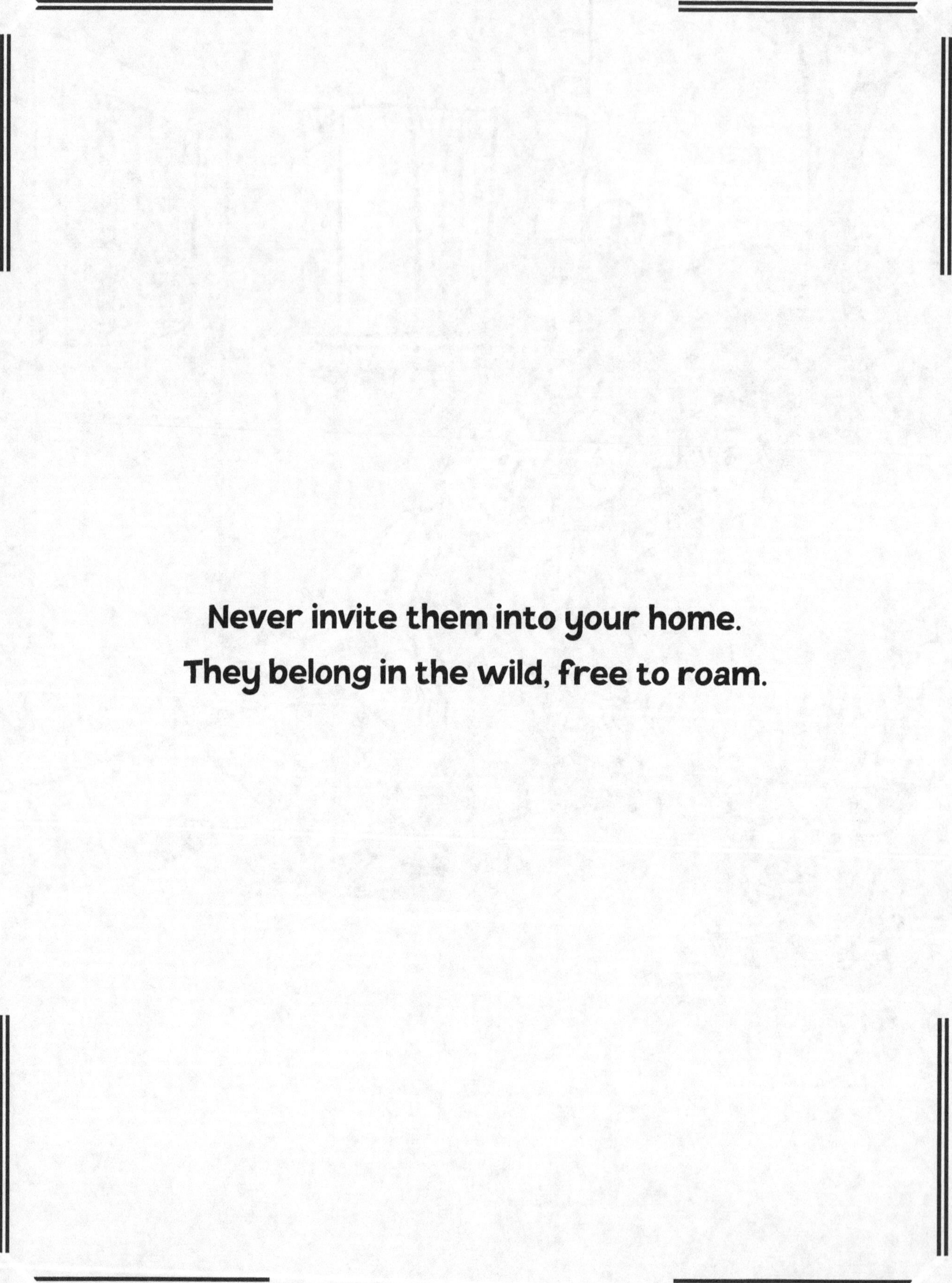

Never invite them into your home.
They belong in the wild, free to roam.

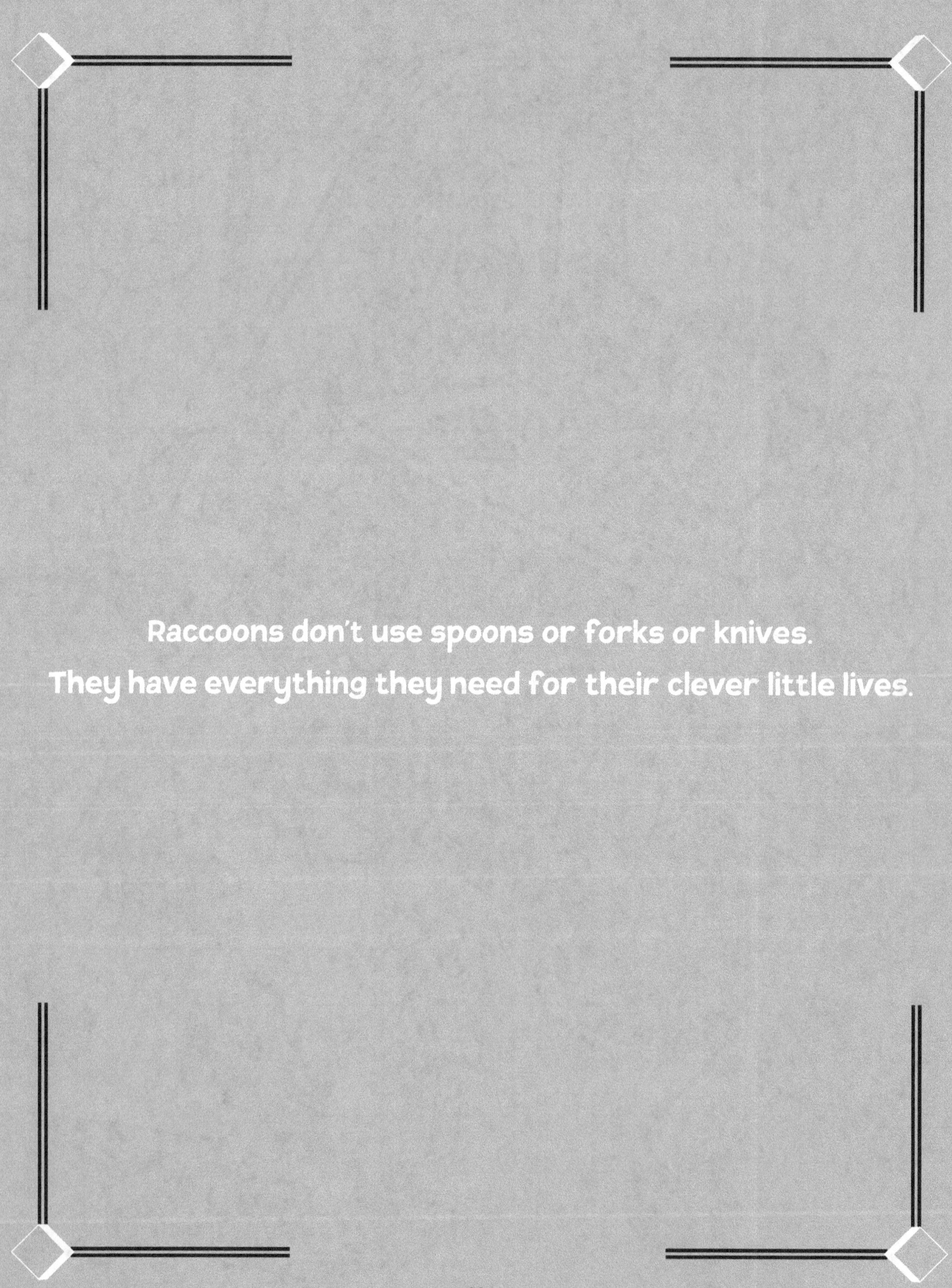

Raccoons don't use spoons or forks or knives.
They have everything they need for their clever little lives.